MY PAPI HAS A MOTORCYCLE

MY PAPI HAS A MOTORCYCLE

Isabel Quintero

illustrated by Zeke Peña

SCHOLASTIC INC.

My papi has a motorcycle.
From him I've learned words like
carburetor and cariño, drill and
dedication.

When I hear his gray truck pull into our driveway,

I run outside with both of our helmets.

THUMP!

THUMP!

My papi, the carpenter, is covered in sawdust and smells like a hard day at work. His hands are rough from building homes every day—his job since he first arrived in this country. But even though he comes home tired he always has time for me.

WOOSHH!

When our city is winding down, he takes me for a ride. Today, he's going to show me the new houses he's working on.

Papi is careful with my ponytail as he pulls my helmet tight.

When he lifts me onto the smooth black seat his hands don't feel rough, they don't feel tired—they feel like all the love he has trouble saying.

Papi revs the engine, and the smell of gasoline hits me as he squeezes the accelerator.

¡CON CUIDADO! BE CAREFUL!

The motor rumbles and growls.

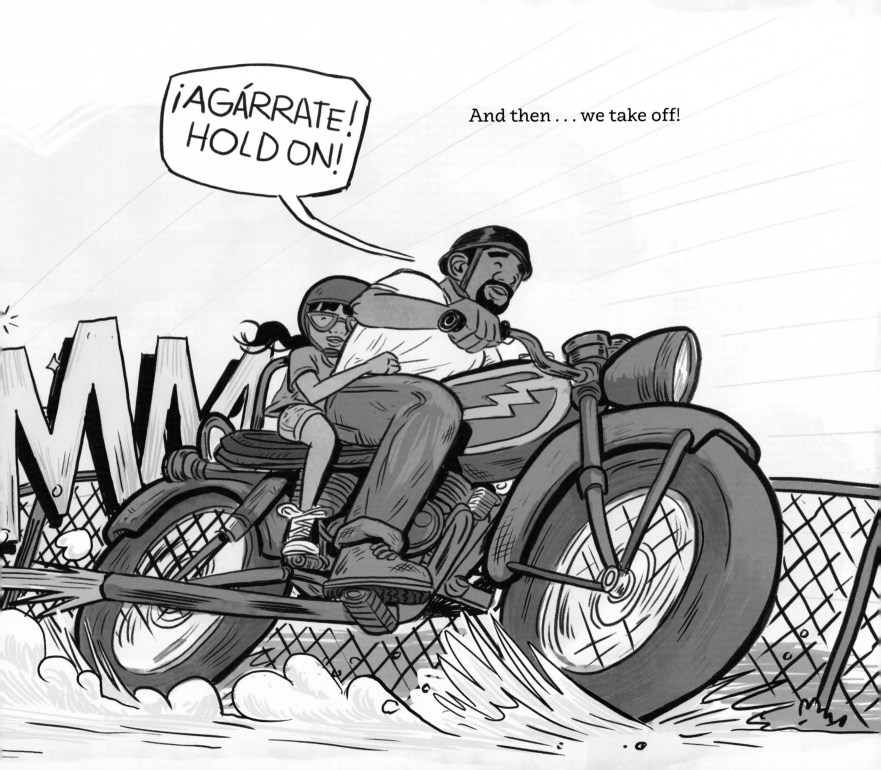

The shiny blue metal of the motorcycle glows in the sun.
The sun, the sun, the bright orange sun is on its way down,
turning our sky blue and purple and gold.
We become a spectacular celestial thing soaring on asphalt.
A comet. The sawdust falling from Papi's hair
and clothes becomes a tail
following us.

Papi zigzags through the streets. We pass Abuelita's church and Tortillería la Estrella and stop for stray cats crossing in front of us. Mami thinks there's too many of them. But I think there's just enough.

We pass Joy's Market where Mami buys my gummy bears.
Mr. García, our librarian, is walking out the door and nods at us.
We nod back. This is how we always greet each other.

We roar past murals that tell our history—
of citrus groves and immigrants who worked them,
and of the famous road race that took place on
Grand Boulevard a hundred years ago.

Now I know that we're stopping at Don Rudy's Raspados.

But as we near the shop, we see that it's empty and out of business.

I can tell Papi is disappointed.

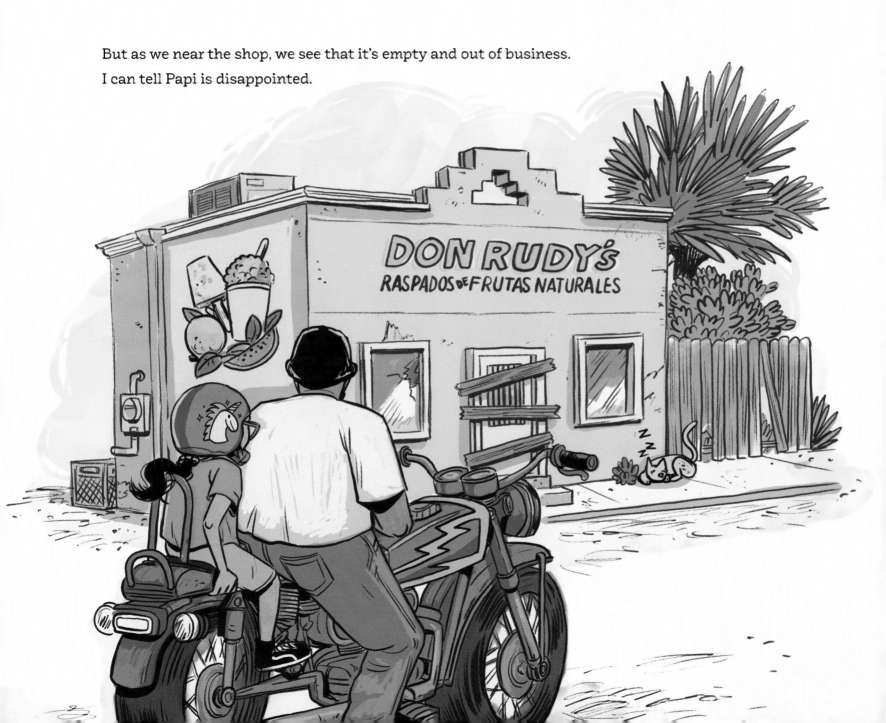

I imagine the smell of the sweet syrups Don Rudy used to flavor our shaved ice.

I won't be the only one who misses him.

CHIRP

CHIRP

CHIRP

As we ride on, I feel and hear everyone and everything we pass by. Each sound landing in my ears rebuilds whole neighborhoods inside me. No matter how far I go from this place, or how much it changes, this city will always be with me.

DING

DING

DING

DING

We cruise by Abuelito and Abuelita's old yellow house—the one with the lemon tree that grew from the seeds of the lemons Abuelito used to pick not far from here. Mami says we're going to visit them tomorrow to cut nopales from their garden and eat herby albóndigas in Abuelita's kitchen, where the food always taste better.

We turn the corner and then . . .

The dogs behind the fences go wild!

WOOF WOOF WOOF WOOF

RUFF

Franky, the Lópezes' Labradoodle, escapes from her yard and runs after us. Mercedes López, the fastest runner in our class, races after her.

Then, just as fast, the dogs barking and Mercedes and Franky become a soft hush in the distance.

We ride toward the new homes replacing the last of the citrus groves.

The painters, drywallers, and floor layers all greet us, but we can barely hear their words amid the sounds of hammers and air compressors.

Even in all that noise, my papi's voice touches everything.

This is my favorite part.

On Grand Boulevard, we lean into the curve of the street. I make believe that we're in one of the races that took place here so long ago! It's our last lap, and we have to win! The crowd cheers us on! I feel Papi's smile as I squeeze my arms tighter around him.

We fly around the circle! There's the school where we practice soccer! There's the post office where Mr. Charlie takes our letters! And la panadería where Papi buys conchas on Sunday mornings!

Here it is, all of our beautiful city!
My eyes try to catch everything, but the colors of houses
blend into one another
redbluegreenorangepink.

We ride, ride, ride until the blue glow from the motorcycle begins to dim, and our comet tail has been left behind on the streets we've traveled. We head home, and slowly the engine echoes us back onto our street and then our driveway— our finish line.

Mami and Little Brother hear the motorcycle and run out to greet us. Mami waves us in, just like a referee. Papi and I can't stop laughing; we had a good ride.

Through our laughter
I hear a familiar sound.

I think about my city and all the changes that it's been through. And all the changes that will come.

But I know that here in our little house,
there are things that will always stay the same.

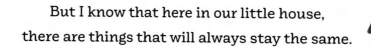

AUTHOR'S NOTE

One of my fondest memories from when I was a little girl is of my apá coming home from work and putting me on the back of his bright blue motorcycle to take a spin around our city, Corona, California. Zeke Peña was able to take all the elements that live in my memory from childhood, even the places that have disappeared like the tortillería and raspado shop, and put them in the illustrations. While the murals he's created are imagined, the history they depict is real. In 1913 Corona held its first road race on what is now Grand Boulevard, a street that makes a perfect circle around the older part of the city. Today, people live in the middle of that old racetrack (I actually grew up there!). At one point in time Corona was also known as the "Lemon Capital of the World" because of all the citrus that was cultivated there. Immigrants did the majority of the hard labor of picking the fruit which allowed for the citrus boom, and this in turn helped establish the city. I wanted to give a nod to the workers who built not only Corona, but a lot of our country, including my grandfather. History and change are always on my mind: Who are the people who build our cities and form our communities? Who are the people who get streets named after them, and who are the people who lay the asphalt? I think these are important questions, and ones I've thought about since I was a kid, and more so as an adult. Ultimately, this book is a love letter to both my father, who showed me different ways of experiencing home, and to Corona, California—a city that will always be a part of me.

Para mi apá.

Para Corona.

–I. Q.

In memory of my Pops.

–Z. P.

ISBN 978-1-338-68601-2

12 11 10 9 8 7 6 5 4 3 2 1   20 21 22 23 24 25

Printed in the U.S.A.   40

First Scholastic printing, September 2020

Text set in Monroe
Design by Jasmin Rubero

The art for this book was created with a Wacom Cintiq 13HD with a mix of hand-painted watercolor texture.

Isabel Quintero

is the daughter of Mexican immigrants. She lives and writes in the Inland Empire of Southern California. Isabel is the author of *Gabi, A Girl in Pieces*, the Ugly Cat & Pablo chapter book series, and was commissioned to write *Photographic: The Life of Graciela Iturbide*, which was awarded the *Boston Globe–Horn Book Award*. One of her favorite memories is riding on the back of her papi's motorcycle as a little girl.

Zeke Peña

is a cartoonist and illustrator working on the United States/Mexico frontera in El Paso, Texas. He makes comics to remix history and reclaim stories using satire and humor; resistencia one cartoon at a time. Zeke studied Art History at the University of Texas Austin and is self-taught in digital illustration. The graphic biography he illustrated titled *Photographic: The Life of Graciela Iturbide*, received the 2018 *Boston Globe–Horn Book* Award.